Wilberforce, Detective

When Wilberforce the whale accidentally arrives in London after a mishap with his new birthday present he is approached by two dapper black cats from the Secret Service and asked to protect the Crown Jewels. With the help of Sid and Flo, two friendly cockney rats, and Hercules, a Thames tug, he hatches a plot. But down at the Tower of London the chums receive a strange warning, and as midnight strikes it becomes obvious that skulduggery is afoot. Can they save the Jewels?

This exciting and amusing story for younger readers or for reading aloud is written by Leslie Coleman, author of *Wilberforce the Whale* and *Wilberforce and the Blue Cave*, also published as Beaver paperbacks.

Wilberforce, Detective

Leslie Coleman

Illustrated by John Laing

Beaver Books

First published in 1975 by Blackie and Son Limited
Bishopbriggs, Glasgow G64 2NZ

This paperback edition published in 1978 by
The Hamlyn Publishing Group Limited
London . New York . Sydney . Toronto
Astronaut House, Feltham, Middlesex, England

© Copyright text Leslie Coleman 1975
© Copyright illustrations on pages 49 and 84
The Hamlyn Publishing Group Limited 1978
Copyright remaining illustrations Blackie and Son Limited 1975
ISBN 0 600 39417 4

Printed in England by Cox & Wyman Limited
London, Reading and Fakenham
Set in Monotype Baskerville

Contents

I

A Hurried Exit

The sun shone down through the water, bright as a birthday sun should, and threw a warm golden glow over the big, flat rock in the middle of the cove. Melody, the shrimp, was swimming around busily – pfut-pfut-pfut-pfut! – setting things out for the party. The centrepiece was a decorated sea-pie of truly birthday dimensions, and round it were ranged clam shells full of seaweed sandwiches, sea-urchin jellies and cuttlefish patties. Just at that moment she was putting final touches to the decorations and trying to persuade a group of brightly coloured sea-anemones to sit round as a border on the rock table.

'I like the Cup Corals best,' she said. 'I think they're even prettier than the Crimson Imperials.'

'Ha-humper-hink-er-happer-er-ha-hoo!' replied Nelson, the crab, scuttling in sideways, his jaws working busily, and waving a piece of chocolate biscuit in one claw.

'Nelson! You haven't started eating already have you?' said Melody, frowning at her small crab friend. 'You mustn't start before they come.'

'Glup!' Nelson gave a great big swallow. 'Those chocolate fingers that fell over the side of that jollyboat this morning – I thought we ought to make sure they were all right.'

'Greedy groats!' Melody laughed.

'But it's such ages to wait, and I'm so excited . . . and so hungry,' complained Nelson.

'It won't be long now,' replied Melody. 'The invitation said, "Tea at four o'clock," and You-know-who is never late for tea. In fact here he is now,' she added, as a large, shadowy bulk started to heave into view down where the bank of braided leaf-weed sloped off into deep water.

'I say!' whispered Nelson. 'Shall we have a joke with him, and hide, and pretend we aren't here? Shall we?'

'That'd be fun,' agreed Melody, 'and we can make him laugh when we jump out.'

And – pish-per-soof! – two little sandstorms whipped up on the sea-bed, and an eyeblink later, no sign remained of shrimp or crab but two tiny hummocks, one on either side of the big, flat rock.

Meanwhile, the large blue-black shape lumbered cheerfully up the hill with casual sweeps of his great fluke tail – per-rump-ah, per-rump-ah! – and as he swam he hummed:

'Happy birthday to me!
Happy birthday to me!
Happy birthday, dear Wilberforce,
Happy birthday to me!'

'Well, here we are then,' beamed the whale, as a final sweep took him into the cove. And then, seeing no one about, 'but on the other hand and contrariwise, where are we? I mean to say, tea's all here – special birthday pie, delicious! – and' (gently nuzzling up the top layer of a sandwich) 'special cuttle-paste sandwiches, my favourite! Most thoughtful! But where is the ship's company? Where, in short, are one's messmates, the merry men, the gang? Now, Miss Melody Shrimp, for instance, are you at home, my shimmy little shoreshaver?'

There was a moment's silence.

'Is there anybody there?' he raised his voice.

'T-ss-ss-ss!' came a suppressed giggle from the further sandy hump.

'Aha!' murmured the whale, with a twinkle in

his eye. 'I dare say my little crackerjack crab friend, Nelson, isn't there either.'

'No!' said the second sand hump.

'So the cove must be quite empty,' murmured Wilberforce, sidling nonchalantly a little towards the nearer hump. 'Quite, quite empty!' he repeated, sidling a little nearer still. 'Quite, quite, absolutely and entirely. . . . Got you!' he cried, pouncing on the Nelson hump.

'And got you, too!' cried the further hump, erupting into a laughing Melody.

'And many happy returns of the day,' cried Melody and Nelson together.

'We've got our presents for you, Wilberforce,' said Nelson, 'but before we give them to you, Melody's got something special to say, one of her chants. Go on, Melody!'

So Melody began:

'Hail! Hail!
   Hail! Hail!
The man of the moment,
   Wilberforce Whale!
Blow on the trumpet and beat on the drum. . . .'

And then Nelson cut in with, 'He's a size fifty mouth and a size ninety tum!'

'Oh Nelson!' wailed Melody. 'That's *not* what

I was going to say, you know it wasn't. The *proper* chant went, "And sing many happy returns to our chum.""

'I think mine's better,' grinned Nelson.

'You cheeky little crab character,' laughed Wilberforce.

'And here's my present,' Nelson continued, producing a piece of cuttlefish tied with an enormous red seaweed bow.

'And mine,' said Melody, handing him a tiny scallop laid out with miniature sea-plants like a garden.

'Oh, thank you,' beamed Wilberforce.

'And *everybody's* coming to the party,' Nelson chattered on excitedly, 'Mr Pout and Stella and Mr Gar and. . . .'

'Whark, whark! Mr Whale, whark?'

Everyone whisked around – per-rump-ah, per-shoot! – at the barked enquiry. They had been so busy with their birthday wishes that they hadn't noticed the new arrival paddling up behind them. At first he looked a little fierce with his two huge tusks jutting downwards from a round face that bristled with whiskers, but then you saw his large brown eyes were really quite friendly.

'Mr Whale, whark?' repeated the walrus, for that is what he was, as he pushed nearer – flop-

flop-flop! – with his two back flippers that seemed somehow to have got tied together.

'Er . . . Mr Whale . . . ?' said Wilberforce, looking about enquiringly. 'Oh! I suppose you mean me!'

'Good! Pleased to meet yer!' barked the walrus. 'Morse, Magnus Morse here! How do, whark!' and he thrust out a leathery flipper to shake hands. 'Now before we get down to the parcel, here's the greetin',' he went on, producing a large birthday card from a deep fold in his fur.

'A present?' asked Wilberforce excitedly.

'That's the rough idea,' replied Mr Morse.

'Oh, what is it? Who's it from? Oh, do let's see!' exclaimed the whale, fumbling to open it out. 'Oh dear! My flippers are all fins! Come on, Nelson, you do it!'

Nelson was almost as excited as his big friend, and shoved his head between the two folds, pushing like a rugby forward to open it out.

At once Wilberforce cried, 'I know the writing. It's from Aunty Barnacle.'

'Your rich, adopted Aunty Barnacle in Scotland?' asked Melody.

'That's it. It'll be the biggest and the best. It always is from Aunty Barnacle. It'll be the best ever! Oh, what is it?'

Mr Morse gave friendly whark and explained, '... Left it down behind the green weed-covered rock! Deeper water ... too shallow to demonstrate here!'

'Come one, then,' shouted Wilberforce, leading the race towards the distant green rock, and – per-rump-ah, per-rump-ah, flop-flop-flop, pfut-pfut-pfut-pfut-pfut! – they all set out to sea.

Of course, poor Melody got left behind in the rush, quite breathless, and all she saw at first was Wilberforce drawing level with the rock and peering behind it. Now, usually when the whale got excited he rushed around in circles and loops like a labrador pup let off the leash, but this time he was so overcome that his body went quite rigid, and then he began to quiver in an ecstasy of delight, from the nub of his nose to the tip of his tail. Then he let out a great shout – 'Wa-ha-roo-ha!' – surged to the surface of the sea – pish-per-soof! – let out a triumphant spout from his blow hole, and sounded vertically – blabble-ebble-ibble-obble-ubble-oompf! – back to the rock.

When at last Melody swam up panting, she could well see why, for there, leaning against the green seaweed rock with fresh black and red paint all picked out in gold lining, was a brand-new, compressed-air, underwater motor bike. Mr Morse was already pointing to the handlebars that Wilberforce would hold in his mouth, to the cylinders of compressed air glistening with power, to the taps and throttles which controlled the flow, and when Melody arrived with Nelson scuttling behind, the Walrus was finishing off with the technical bits about 'self-adjusting return-valves, pressure ratios and inlet controls,' and Wilberforce was looking very wise indeed.

And then Mr Morse said, 'Well, I think that's the lot. How about a try? Don't forget, lever this way for "easy", upright for "half-speed" and right over for "full-power", and if you push the red button, you get two cylinders at once and go off like a rocket. I'll just show you.'

With one practised tusk Mr Morse nudged the lever, nodded the handlebars with the other, and – pr-rr-rr-ush-sh! – made a little circle round the green seaweed rock.

'Now you try!' he barked, dismounting.

So Wilberforce climbed on and, with Mr Morse running beside him, made a fair but rather more wobbly circle – per-ush-er-oosh-per-per-per-er-oosh! – And then Melody and Nelson sat on the handlebars, and Mr Morse took them for quite a fast ride – pr-rr-ush-sh-sh-sh! – and even looped the loop.

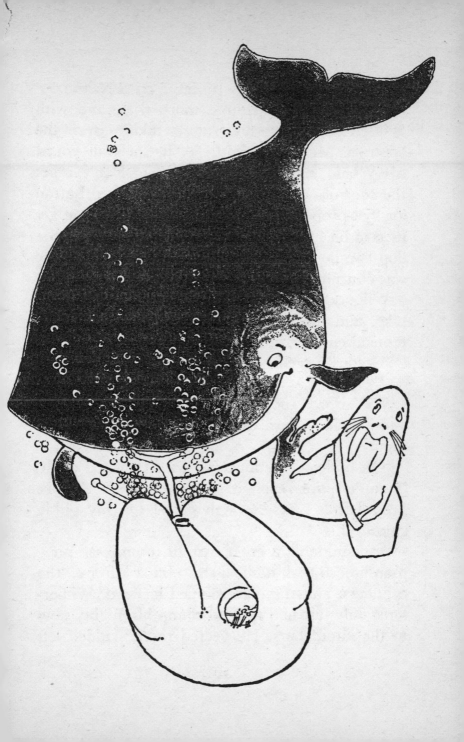

'Oo-ooh! I've lost my tummy,' cried Nelson.

At last, after a couple more tries, and with Wilberforce more and more taking over the controls, Mr Morse said, 'Well, she's all yours, Mr Whale. Easy as falling off a log! Don't forget the controls – the lever for "normal", red button for "jet-propelled", but I'd leave that till you get used to her. Good luck! Good-bye, whark!' and – flop-flop-flop – Mr Morse's double back flipper was churning him off the way he had come.

Wilberforce lay gazing, entranced, at his new bike, and his heart thumped so that he hardly remembered to return the 'Good-bye!'

'Go on!' urged Nelson, 'Show us what you can do.'

Wilberforce took the handlebars in his mouth and reached towards the control with his left flipper.

'Oh bother!' he muttered with clenched teeth, 'I can't quite reach it. Now ... yes, that's it. Press left ... yes ... Oh golly! Oh my giddy galoshes!'

And suddenly a great rush of compressed air – proosh-oosh-oosh-oosh-sh-sh! burst from the cylinders, and the bike zoomed forward. Wilberforce only just had time to clamp his mighty jaws to the handlebars. He veered right, skidded left and rocketed so close to Melody that she squealed:

'Oh, Wilberforce!'

'Cor!' cried Nelson in admiration.

Then, jet-propelled, the whale was hurtling straight out into the darkness of the deep, deep sea.

Wilberforce had touched the *red* button by mistake!

2

Wilberforce Goes to Town

The machine raced forward headlong, with such terrific speed that Wilberforce simply shut his eyes and clung on. Of course, he realised that if he only let go of the handlebars he could drop astern and swim home easily, but that would mean losing his brand-new birthday bike, which was quite unthinkable. So he gritted his teeth and hoped there wasn't too much gas in the double cylinder.

The cries of 'Stop! Come back! ... Wilberforce, come back!' from Melody and Nelson had scarcely died away behind him, when they were replaced by another sound – per-r-omp, er-r-omp, er-r-omp! – and through the green half-light of water, Wilberforce saw a vast, shadowy hull looming up ahead. It was so long that its stern was way, way out of sight, and it was running on a direct collision course.

'Crikey-go-lightly!' muttered the whale through clenched teeth. 'It's an oil tanker *and* – suffering swordfish! – going at full speed!'

With all his strength he wrestled the stubborn handlebars and just managed to inch them to one side, veering away in the last second from disaster under the mighty tanker's bows.

But no sooner had he done that, than – per-romp, er-r-omp, er-r-omp! – the keel of a freighter, rusty red, came ploughing along in the other direction.

Wilberforce gasped and curved his great fluke tail downwards, trying to use it as a brake, but – shivering sharks! – the bike was going so fast that it hardly made any difference. He only just cleared the propeller, and the shock waves twisted him round and round like a corkscrew, over and over and over and over and over. Then even before he could recover his breath, another ship, a collier, came churning on a cross-track and, though Wilberforce tried to pull away to one side, it caught him a glancing blow.

Next, another ship dashed by to port and another rolled him over to starboard. But *still* he clung on to the runaway bike, doing his best to twist and steer away, as ships of all shapes and sizes seemed to be coming at him from every quarter. It was just as if they were wasps and he had disturbed their nest.

'This is pandemonium!' Wilberforce panted. 'A navigator's nightmare! Oh my giddy – *help*!' he cried, but alas it was too late. An unseen coaster cut right across his course and hit him – wump! – full on the nose.

Stars flashed, his ears buzzed and everything went muzzy. Somehow he had an odd sense that instead of floating in the sea, he was way, way up above the clouds. . . .

The next thing that Wilberforce knew was that he was on the surface. He kept his eyes shut because his head was still ringing, and he could feel a large lump coming up on his nose. But far more important than all this, he realised that he was lying still. The bike had run out of gas!

Then a hoarse but not unfriendly voice said:

'Haw-aw, haw-aw! My name's Haw-aw, Hercules. What's your-haw-aw name, wha-ale?'

Wilberforce opened one eye. A light summer mist had descended, and he was riding on an olive-green sea. Just a couple of cables to starboard was a tubby tar-black tug with a dumpy red funnel. It was almost as broad as it was long, and painted in bold white letters across its stern were the words, *Hercules – London*.

'I'm Wilberforce,' replied the whale.

'Haw-aw-hello, Wilberfor-orce, then!' said Hercules in his foghorn voice. 'Isn't this a glorious mist?'

'I don't think I'm very fond of fogs at sea,' replied the whale. 'They're dangerous for shipping, you know.'

'Haw-aw-aw *I* like them haw-awfully. It's only when there's a good thick mist that I'm allowed to talk. When it's fine they only let me say dull things like, "Haw, haw, haw! I'm going astern," but I can talk as much as I like when it's foggy. That's a haw-horrid bump you have on your-haw nose. Does it haw-hurt very much?'

'It does a bit. Thank you kindly for asking,' Wilberforce replied rather ruefully.

'Well, come alongside, matey, and let's see what we can do to 'elp,' cut in a chipper cockney voice, and out from the coils of a very thick rope which nearly filled Hercules's after-deck, darted a furry rat. His eyes were sharp and humorous, and his nose and whiskers positively twinkled.

The rat sprang on to the taffrail at the back of the tug and looked down at the bump as Wilberforce eased over – per-rump-ah! – under his own power.

'Cor! That ain't 'alf a beauty,' the rat continued, eyeing Wilberforce's battered nose. 'That ain't no pigeon's egg wot you got there, mate; that ain't no duck's egg; that there's a h'ostrich egg!' Then, 'Flo!' called the little animal, and almost at once another cheery, furry rat, rather plumper but still very active, jumped on the rail beside him.

'Flo!' the first rat continued, 'nip across to the galley and see if cook'll give you a pat of butter, there's a duck. . . . Wunnerful stuff, butter, for smoothin' bumps!'

'Thanks very much indeed,' said Wilberforce. 'That's very kind of you Mister er . . . er . . .!'

'Sid,' put in the rat promptly, 'Sidney's the monica, and 'er,' he went on, pointing to the departing figure of his plump partner, ''er, that's Flo. She and me, we got spliced on this very coil of rope. She's a real China.'

'Er, China?' queried Wilberforce, puzzled.

'China plate . . . mate . . . get it? Flo's me mate, so I calls her my China plate . . . me China. . . .'

'Oh, I see,' laughed Wilberforce, 'it rhymes, and then you leave out the rhyming bit, and you've got a sort of private language that only *you* can understand!'

'That's it. Rhyming slang they calls it. Nah this tug wot we're on, he's called 'Ercules. 'E ain't very sharp, but. . . .'

'Haw-aw!' put in Hercules, 'My bows are as sharp as the next boat's. Haw-who does all the work round here, haw-aw, while you passengers get all the haw-halfpence, haw-aw?'

'No offence, 'Erky-boy!' put in Sid quickly. 'Just pulling your leg!'

'And I suppose he's a China too,' said Wilberforce. 'But he looks a bit solid to be made of china, ha-ha-ha!' And Hercules also seemed to enjoy the little joke, for he went literally into hoots of laughter – Haw-aw, haw-aw, haw-aw, haw-aw, haw-aw!

'See wot I mean,' said Sid, "e likes 'is jokes simple. And he only talks in a fog. When the sun's out – not a dicky!'

'Dicky?' said Wilberforce, and then, 'Oh of course, that's rhyming slang too. Now don't tell me; let me guess. Dicky . . . dicky . . . dicky. . . . I've got it! Dicky *bird* – means *word*! He doesn't say a dicky means he doesn't speak a word.'

Sid laughed in agreement.

'Oh, 'e's a right one,' he said to Flo as she hurried back with a large lump of butter in her mouth. 'Yer-ers indeed! Ain't never 'eard rhyming slang before, but 'e's pickin' it up like lightning.'

'It'll be like *greased* lightning when I got this on 'is bump,' laughed Flo as she skipped off the taffrail on to Wilberforce's back and padded forward with the butter to the tip of his nose. There she squatted down and started to ease the grease gently on to the hurt bit with her forepaws.

'Oh, that's very soothing, thank you, Flo,' said the whale and, while Flo massaged the butter ointment in, he told them all about his birthday, and the runaway bike, and the awful shipping, and his bump.

'And now,' he concluded, 'I'm completely lost. Please, where are we?'

'Well, that wot you come up, mate,' said Sid, is called the Channel. All the ships in the world get there. Like bloomin' Piccadilly! Not surprised you got a bump! Ought to 'ave traffic lights, they ought! Look right, look left, look right and listen – you know the drill! And then 'alf the boats'ld want a lollipop man to see 'em through!'

'And so, if I want to go back . . .' Wilberforce hesitated.

'It's back through all that lot,' said Sid. Then, seeing Wilberforce's worried look, he added, 'But why *go* back? Come on up to town and stay with us.'

'Show you all the sights,' put in Flo hospitably. 'Changing the Guard, hot dogs, St Paul's, moving staircases, the lot!'

'And the haw-aw-Houses of Parliament!' put in Hercules.

'Oh-oh!' said Wilberforce. 'To go up to town!' he thought. 'To see the Houses of Parliament, perhaps even the Queen!' he thought. What tales he would have to tell Melody and Nelson and all his friends back at the cove! 'Oh, *yes* thanks,' said Wilberforce, 'Yes, thank you very much!'

'Well then you put that bike o' yours aboard,' said Sid, lowering a rope, 'and we'll get the skids on.'

Then Hercules gave a 'haw-aw, haw-aw, haw-aw' on his hooter to warn other ships they were coming, and off they set with Wilberforce swimming comfortably alongside – per-rump-ah, per-rump-ah, per-rump-ah! – and very soon the mist lifted, and a glorious pink and pearly-grey evening set in across the mud-flats of the great estuary.

Wilberforce was so enthusiastic about his visit to London that he started to sing in his rumbling voice:

'Half a pound of tuppenny rice.
Pom-ty, pom-ty, treacle. . . .'

''Old it!' cried Sid, 'if you want to sing, we'll lend a 'and.'

And he and Flo got out spoons which they played like castanets, and Hercules came in on the bass notes.

'Up and down the City Road,' sang Sid.

'In and out The Eagle,' replied Flo.

And then everyone chimed in at once:

'That's the way the money goes.'

And Hercules rounded it off with a deep bass, 'Haw-aw-aw! goes the weasel.'

In this way they passed up the Thames, scarcely noticing mud-flats, piers, oil installations, power houses, factories or housing estates, until suddenly Wilberforce realised they were in the heart of a great city. The peaks of cranes soared above warehouses, and through locks and entrances could be glimpsed masts and funnels of moored ships.

Tugs and rafts of barges passed up and down, and despite the absence of fog, Hercules and his friends got very chatty indeed:

'Haw-aw-aw-aw!'

'He-he-he!'

'Her-erp, her-erp!'

'Ha-ah, ha-ah, ha-ah!'

And so they went on, until suddenly their way was blocked by a great bridge. It was flanked by two tall towers joined by a great girder high up in the sky, and across the bridge hooted and skirled taxis and giant buses, and humans and private cars in a stream even busier than the river traffic.

'That's Tower Bridge,' explained Sid.

At that moment, Hercules turned sharply towards the left bank and a raft of barges.

'Well, welcome 'ome,' said Sid. 'This is it. It mayn't be much, but it's all we got, and we bids yer a 'earty welcome.'

3

The Mysterious Assignment

The evening sun was already touching the roofs of the city offices as Hercules puffed alongside the raft of barges. They were moored at the end of a long jetty, and the stern hawser had barely been made fast before Sid was scuttering half-way down it, followed more sedately by Flo. A jump and a skip took them on to the first barge, called *Primrose*, which was lying low in the water under a heavy load of coal, and another jump carried them aboard her twin sister, *Bella*.

"Erky takes the gals up to the power station most days, just for the run,' explained Sid. 'Keeps their figures in trim.'

And then another skip took him and Flo on to the third barge.

'And this is us,' he cried.

'Us' was a lighter with the plain inscription on its stern: *J. F. Hogband and Co.* At first Wilberforce couldn't decide what made J. F. Hogband different. True, his decks were scrupulously clean, his brasswork polished and his hold neatly shuttered. But it was only when the whale found his nose twitching that he realised that it was the smell, the rather pleasant, aromatic smell of cinnamon, nutmeg and ginger, that marked Mr Hogband as an individual apart.

'J.F.H., he's in hexport-himport,' said Sid. 'Works the h'East India docks.'

What on earth 'hexport–himport' might be, Wilberforce had no idea, but the East India docks certainly explained the jolly smell.

'He's ever-so comfy,' put in Flo, 'all soft sacks and bales inside.'

'J.F.H. 'as just got back from the ware'ouse with a fresh load,' said Sid. 'So if it's all the same to you, me and Flo'd like to get down them apples and pears. . . .'

'Stairs?' suggested Wilberforce with a grin.

'You're getting it, matey! We'd like to get below and see what's what. You never know what little treat J.F.H. mayn't 'ave aboard. We shan't be 'alf a jiffy.'

And the two rats scuttered off down the companionway, and at the same time, Hercules gave a great big yawn.

'Haw-aw! I'm half asleep already,' he said.

Then – Sh-sh-sh-sh-sh! – letting off what steam was left, he settled down for the night.

Wilberforce lay alone, drinking it all in. Opposite lay the docks, and there to his left, through the great bridge, was the Tower of London itself. The four-square keep with turrets at each corner was touched to a rosy pink by the setting sun. The whale's heart swelled with excitement. This was the city, the *real* city, and he felt he wanted to be a part of the very scene itself.

'A hat!' he thought. 'That's what I want!'

Now his Aunty Barnacle had taught him a Celtic rune to make them. So although it was rather cramped and shallow, he wriggled under Bella (for it had to be done in secret), and muttered the special rhyme:

'Leg of toad and wing of bat
Make a new and natty hat!'

'... Something appropriate to the City,' he muttered, concentrating very hard. Then there was the usual crisp little 'ching', and Wilberforce surfaced again – blubble-obble-ibble-ebble-abble-sfish!

He lay a moment, admiring his own reflection in the water.

'A top-hat, the very thing!' he murmured. '*And* a monocle!' Now he felt properly equipped to meet the City Fathers, the Prime Minister, or even to bow over a Royal hand!

'Ps-ss-ss!' said a voice behind him.

Wilberforce turned as fast as he could in the shallow water – per-oosh-er-oosh! – and came face to face with two black cats lounging along the jetty. One of them wore a bowler hat, and the other carried an umbrella. The one with the umbrella looked down at Wilberforce with jade slit eyes in a thoughtful sort of way and then, turning to his companion, said, 'A fish that wears a top hat and a monocle must be a very superior sort of a fish. Do you think, dear fellah, that he might perhaps be the answer to our problem?'

'You mean to effect the surveillance from the river by means of a large, intelligent sea monster?' replied the other. 'Plausible, old boy, very plausible!'

Wilberforce coughed.

'Excuse me,' he said, 'but I am *not* a fish. I am a whale, a mammal, and I breathe air like you,' and by way of demonstration he blew a small fountain of air and water from his blow-hole.

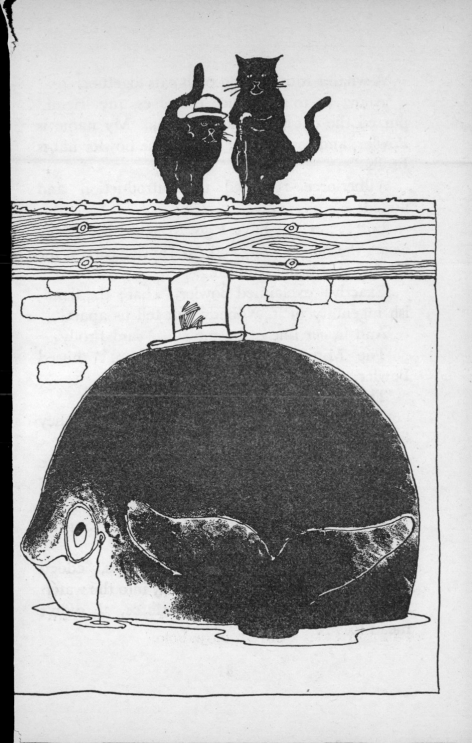

'A whale! Ideal!' cried both cats together.

'Allow us to introduce ourselves, my friend,' purred the cat with the umbrella. 'My name is Bowler, and my partner here in the bowler hat is Brolly.'

Wilberforce returned the introduction and added:

'But ... er ... have I got it right? Mr Brolly wears the bowler hat, and Mr Bowler carries the brolly? It's rather confusing.'

'Exactly!' exclaimed Bowler. 'That's the fiend-ish ingenuity of it. Nobody can tell us apart!'

'And in *our* line of business . . .' said Brolly.

'The Ministry, you understand . . .' hissed Bowler.

'The Service . . .' whispered Brolly.

'The Sh-sh-sh, you'd-never-guess-who!' they finished in chorus.

'You don't mean,' said Wilberforce, his eyes opening wide, 'you don't mean the *Secret* Service!'

'Sh-sh-sh!' both cats spluttered together.

'We never mention it,' said Brolly, looking up at the sky distantly.

'Such a word never passes our lips,' added Bowler looking down impenetrably into the water.

'Oh, I'm sorry,' said Wilberforce, 'I didn't mean to. . . .'

'Not to worry, my friend!' said Brolly, gazing at a passing bird. 'I don't expect that seagull could really hear you.'

'Probably one of ours, anyway!' said Bowler. 'Pray pardon us, dear lad, if we have a small conference.'

And the two cats put their heads close together and started whispering – ps-ss-ss, ps-ss-ss-fish, ps-ss-ss-wilber, pss-ss-force, ps-ss-ss! – with frequent glances over their shoulders at Wilberforce, which made him feel rather embarrassed. Finally they both turned round.

'There's no doubt about it, dear lad,' they both purred together. 'You're the one.'

'Intelligent!' Brolly breathed.

'Strong!' Bowler beamed.

'Observant!'

'And above all . . . not generally known in the area.'

'In short, the ideal person!' As usual, the two cats concluded in chorus.

'Old man,' Brolly edged earnestly towards him, 'as an honest sea citizen, can we count on you in a . . . very delicate matter?'

'Why, certainly! Anything!' replied Wilberforce, much flattered at their approach. 'What do you want me to do?'

'Ps-ss-ss!' whispered Bowler and Brolly together, beckoning him to the end of the jetty where they could whisper right into his ear.

'A mendicant mullah of Mandragore . . .' began Bowler in a very confidential whisper.

'Has told a beggar in Baghdad . . .' went on Brolly holding his hat to his face to prevent anyone overhearing these state secrets.

'Who reported to our cat in Constantinople. . . .'

'Who forwarded a dispatch by diplomatic balloon to Paris. . . .'

'Who naturally sent an express pigeon post to. . . .'

'Ps-ss-ss!' they concluded together, 'We can't say who!'

'But what was the secret news?' urged Wilberforce, quivering with excitement and curiosity.

'Do we tell our friend?' Brolly turned to Bowler.

'I think we must,' replied Bowler opening his umbrella so as to hide the three of them completely. '. . . The Crown Jewels!' he muttered out of the corner of his mouth.

'The Crown Jewels?' echoed Wilberforce.

Brolly nodded.

'An international gang of thieves is planning to steal the Crown and Sceptre!'

'From the Tower of London!'

'That very fortress that you see on the far side of good, honest Old Father Thames!'

Wilberforce glanced across under Tower Bridge at the grey stone walls of the Keep. They looked terribly strong and safe.

'That very tower!' Brolly went on. '*You* must prevent it.'

'Me!' gasped the whale.

'If you refuse, think of the effect upon the nation!'

'Disastrous!'

'Catastrophic!'

'Law and order destroyed!'

'Strikes!'

'Riots!'

'Her Majesty unable to leave Buckingham Palace!'

'The plot *must* be defeated,' they hissed urgently together.

'We need an undercover man,' Bowler pressed.

'We need *you*, Mr Whale,' concluded Brolly, and his jade eyes opened wide like green fire and then closed to narrow slits.

'Well, I'm not a trained detective,' said Wilberforce modestly, 'but if you think. . . .'

'That's settled then,' said Bowler, and – ps-ss-ss! – both cats disappeared, just like a conjuring trick. A second later two heads appeared, one on either side of a bollard.

'Secret instructions will reach you in due course,' hissed Bowler.

'In the meantime – not to tell a soul!' added Brolly. 'Ps-ss-ss! You don't know who may be listening!'

And – ps-ss-ss! – both cats finally disappeared.

Wilberforce lay there for a moment, quite breathless. To have become a private detective! And for his first case a confidential government assignment! What would his secret instructions be? Perhaps he ought to start getting his detective outfit together. He would need a magnifying glass for sure. . . .

'Right you are then, matey,' Sid's voice cut in on his reverie. 'Flo's just bringing up the grub. Wot you got, Flo?'

'Saffron rice and Bombay duck,' puffed his plump mate dragging a big sack behind her.

'Suit you, Wilberforce boy?'

'Oh! . . . er . . . er, anything you like,' replied Wilberforce, who was away off in a dazed dream.

'Thought I heard you talking to somebody while we were down in the hold.'

'Oh yes,' Wilberforce brightened. 'Two very important. . . .'

'Ps-ss-ss!' came a voice from behind the bollard.

'Two very friendly people asked . . . er . . . if I knew where the Tower was,' he concluded lamely.

'Oh!' said Sid, and the conversation lapsed.

For some time they ate in silence. Then Sid looked at Flo and winked.

'P'raps we're all ready for bed,' he said, and indeed, lights had already started to twinkle in the office windows and across Tower Bridge.

Wilberforce nodded. He wanted to be alone to think.

'Well, there's a deep trench underneath J.F.H., so you won't be stranded when the tide drops. I think you'll find it quite comfy.'

'Oh er . . . yes,' replied Wilberforce absently. 'Thank you!'

'Sleep tight!' called Flo.

But in his excited frame of mind, it was going to be a long time before Wilberforce got to sleep.

4

Hercules to the Rescue

Wilberforce woke with a start. He was surprised at first to find himself in the narrow trench underneath J. F. Hogband's keel, but soon recalled the adventures of the previous day. Warm sun filtered down through the water to announce a glorious morning up above, and so he didn't hesitate when he heard Sid's perky voice:

'What ho, below there, matey! Sun's up! Show a fin!'

Blubble-ubble, obble-obble, ibble-ebble-abble, swoosh! – Wilberforce surfaced into one of those delicious April days, when the grass is all sprinkled with dew, and you can simply *smell* spring everywhere.

'Has the postman been?' was Wilberforce's first query, hoping that perhaps his secret instructions might have come.

'Nah,' said Sid, 'we don't 'ave much call for the post out 'ere.'

The young rat was squatting on the after-deck, brushing his whiskers and admiring his reflection in J.F.H.'s shiny brass registration plate.

'Cor! You wasn't 'alf "asleep in the deep" mate,' Sid laughed. 'I been calling you a good five minutes.'

Flo came scuttling up the companionway, bright and breezy.

'Mornin', all!' she said. "Ow about a cup of Rosie Lea?' and she tilted a huge pot towards three tin mugs.

'Tea!' said Wilberforce. 'Very comforting, thanks!'

'My!' Flo went on, eyeing Wilberforce's topper and monocle, which she noticed for the first time in daylight. 'My! Aren't we grand this morning!'

'Yus,' put in Sid, 'I rather fancy the gear my-self – that old silk titfer and all!'

'Titfer?' queried Wilberforce. 'Oh, tit-for-tat – the hat! I thought I might swim up to the Houses of Parliament and raise it to the members – just as a gesture, you know. The monocle is extra, of course, a little touch, but er . . . dashing, I felt, er er . . . imposing not to say *distingué*.'

'Oh, 'ighly h'appropriate!' replied Sid, "Ighly

h'appropriate! Now why I called you was seein' as 'ow 'Erky boy here 'as got to run the gals up to the power station, me and Flo thought we'd go along just for the ride. 'Ow about you, Wilby boy?'

'I feel a bit lazy,' replied Wilberforce. 'I shall be quite happy hanging around J.F.H. until you get back. There's such a lot to look at.' The whale felt he *had* to be on hand in case his secret instructions came.

'Righty-ho then,' said Sid. 'See you later!'

Hercules threw off his mooring lines, hitched Bella and Primrose side by side on his tow and put his nose out into the river.

'Ha-a-a-ave a good ti-i-i-ime!' he hooted and set off up-stream with Flo and Sid waving over the taffrail.

They were still in sight, and Wilberforce was just watching to see them disappear under the bridge, when – 'ps-ss-ss!' – he heard someone trying to attract his attention on the jetty. Full of excitement, he spun round – per-roosh! As he had half expected, Brolly's bowler-hatted head was looking round the bollard.

'Good morning, Mr Brolly,' Wilberforce said politely. Then, dropping into an appropriate whisper, 'Have you brought my secret inst . . .?'

'Ps-ss-ss!' interrupted the cat. 'You-never-know who is giving the orders!'

'But today you would be well advised,' said Bowler appearing on the other side of the bollard, 'to have a swim around. . . .'

'Get to know your parish,' added Brolly.

'Size up the situation and so on!' concluded Bowler vaguely waving his umbrella.

'Meanwhile – ps-ss-ss! – not a word to a soul! You never know who may be listening,' And – pfut! – their two heads disappeared behind the bollard.

Wilberforce was delighted with their suggestion and, cocking his topper at a rakish angle, set off at once on a jaunt of exploration. Leaving the docks on his right, he headed for the mist of feathery buds surrounding the trees on Tower Green, which he could see through the bridge. As he did so he noticed a removal van crossing the roadway at the end of a line of traffic, and this prompted him to burst into one of his cheerful bumbles:

> 'My old man said, "Follow the van
> Don't dilly-dally ompty pom!" he sang.
> 'Om-pom-pom. . . .'

But at this point he stopped short. For the

bridge was empty. Nothing had crossed after the removal van. The hustling, bustling, honking, hooting stream of traffic had dried up, and the lower span lay quite silent. Then, slowly and steadily, the great bridge started to divide in the middle, and its two massive arms lifted upwards and outwards like two drawbridges, leaving the river open for traffic. Then, slow and stately from the Upper Pool, a big merchantman slid through the gap, on the flood, making for the estuary and the open sea.

For a moment Wilberforce's jaw dropped in wonder at the majestic sight. Then he realised he must clear the fairway if he wasn't to be run down, and made a quick dash – per-rump-ah, per-rump-ah, per-rump-ah! – for the near bank, and before he had fully recovered his breath, the ship had passed, the bridge had closed again and, when at last he swam underneath, traffic was once more rumbling over the top.

Wilberforce ploughed cheerfully on, swimming on the surface of the dark stream whose wavelets reflected the warm sun like dancing diamonds. Three bridges later the apple-green buds of the trees on the Embankment framed his view, and a sparrow fluttering a yard or two offshore perched cheekily on his head with a chirruped: 'Good morning! Good morning! Good morning!'

'And a sparkling "Good morning!" to you, my spicky little sparrow friend,' Wilberforce laughed back. And the spring sunshine was so infectious that he started rumbling another of his old favourites, though the words seemed to have got a bit changed:

'Tra-la, la-la-la, la-la-la-la, la-la, ti-diddle-do!
A detective's lot's a *very* cheerful one!
Pom-ti-pom!'

... and the 'pom-ti-pom' was so hearty that the little sparrow was bounced right up into the air.

'Cor blimey! It's like trying to roost on an ogo-pogo stick!' complained the little cockney bird.

'It's the spring that does it,' replied Wilberforce, and they both burst out laughing.

In the next reach, the whale at last found himself opposite the great Gothic tower of Big Ben and the grey buttressed buildings of the Houses of Parliament. One or two gentlemen, probably M.P.s, were taking 'elevenses' on the terrace which overlooked the river, and Wilberforce turned with awe to stare at these important personages. But what he didn't realise was that *they* had turned in awe to stare at *him*.

Indeed, Wilberforce's presence in the Thames had not by any means passed unnoticed on the human plane.

'WHALE IN TOP-HAT CRUISES OFF WESTMINSTER,' read the headlines of the mid-morning papers, and the Honourable Member for Wapping Steps had asked the Minister for the Navy, '... Whether he was aware that this House was being quizzed at that very instant by an unidentified whale wearing a monocle, and what did he propose to do about it?'

People were lining bridges to stare, in the hopes of getting a glimpse of the strange phenomenon. The big red buses on the Embankment stopped, as everyone peered from the upper deck in astonishment at the sight of the whale who wore a monocle and top hat.

And Wilberforce swam jauntily on upstream, totally unaware of the furore he was creating, quietly enjoying the spring air and the chirpy companionship of his little cockney sparrow friend. So it was several minutes before he realised that creeping up behind him were four . . . five . . . *six* . . . *seven* . . . *eight* launches riding abreast, and all intent on catching the whale in the top hat!

There was a boat from the Zoo, who wanted to put him in a tank. There was a boat from the Customs, who wanted to know if he had anything to declare. There was a boat from TV, who wanted to take his picture; and a boat from a newspaper, who wanted to know what he thought of the latest spring fashions; and there was a boat from the Police, who said that he was exceeding the speed limit; and there was even a boat from a museum who wanted to put him in a glass case! But they all had one thing in common – *they wanted to catch him*! And it was not till they were within yards that poor Wilberforce had an inkling of what was going on.

Then the chase began in earnest. The river held too little water for Wilberforce to sound, so he did the next best thing and did a shallow dive. But still his threshing flukes left a tell-tale stream of bubbles to show where he was. Per-rump-ah, per-rump-ah, per-rump-ah! – he went, and – br-rr-rm, br-rr-rm, br-rr-rm! – went the motor launches. And their bow waves built up, and their combined wash ran *ten feet high* along the stone walls of the bank! Wilberforce strained with all his might – per-rump-ah, per-rump-ah! – but still the boats were inching up on him. Some of them were already getting out their nets because they thought they would soon be near enough to catch him ... and one even had a *harpoon*! Wilberforce could feel a sort of pricking up and down his spinc, as he realised that soon he must tire, whilst his pursuers had power and petrol for half a day.

And then came the sound which brought him to the surface – haw-aw, haw-aw! – and, oh blessed hope! – it was Hercules returning with Primrose and Bella, now riding high in the water after discharging their cargo of coal at the power station.

Wilberforce blew a great spout from his blow-hole, to attract the tubby tug's attention, and it wasn't long before Hercules sized up the situation.

'Haw-aw, haw-aw!' he hooted. 'Move across to port a bit.' Then, 'Hoo-ha, hoo-ha, hoo! . . . Make a big circle to turn downstream . . .' and, 'ha-aw, ha-aw, ha-aw! . . . Come in, astern of my tow.'

Wilberforce grasped the plan at once and put on a tremendous spurt with his mighty fluke tail – per-rump-ah, per-rump-ah! – thrashing the water into a Niagara of foam, and he forged ahead so swiftly that for a moment he left his pursuers right behind. Then, as he met Hercules coming straight downstream towards him, he edged slightly over to port, dived, made a light-ning half turn under water and shot in astern of the tug under the blessed shelter of Bella and Primrose, where he was completely hidden from the dreaded hunter boats who wanted to make him a prisoner.

As he swam in under the keels of the two barges, an anchor was lowered on the end of a rope, and on to the anchor was hooked . . . his bike! Sid and Flo had not only thought to let it down for him, but had coupled up a new cylinder of compressed air.

This time, Wilberforce was careful to press the

proper lever. And so it was, that with the handle-bars of his birthday bike safely gripped in his jaws, and no wave from his fluke tail to give his position away, the great whale rode to safety, right through the ranks of his enemies.

'MYSTERY OF DISAPPEARING WHALE!' read the evening papers' headline. 'IS HE A FOREIGN AGENT IN DISGUISE? PUBLIC ENQUIRY DEMANDED.'

Meanwhile Wilberforce lay, a little breathless but otherwise unscathed, in the trench under J.F.H.'s keel, still waiting for his secret instructions.

5

An Impenetrable Disguise

'The bother, dear boy,' said Bowler, 'is the hat.'

'The topper, you see,' added Brolly.

'Please don't get us wrong, dear friend,' Bowler went on. 'For Ascot or the Royal Garden Party. . . .'

'Just the thing, perhaps even more so. . . .'

'But for a detective on duty . . .!'

The cats had appeared, slithering down the single standard lamp at the end of the jetty just as its one naked bulb had flickered on. Wilber-force was lying on the surface breathing, after spending most of the afternoon under J.F.H.'s keel, and a thin crescent moon rising over the roofs of Limehouse Reach gave a pale half-light, where you couldn't be certain whether this shape or that was a shadow, a rat, or a coil of rope.

The cats landed with two soft 'flumps', Brolly

first and then Bowler, holding his umbrella between his teeth like a pirate carrying a knife down the rigging.

'What is required, dear friend . . .' Bowler went on.

'The er *desiderata* . . .' put in his colleague.

'Is something a little less . . . how shall I put it. . .?'

'Or, in other words, something a little more. . . .'

Kitch-er, kitch-er, kitch! – a menacing snicker interrupted them – kitch-er, kitch! – and it came from the direction of J. F. Hogband's deck.

In the shadow, Flo and Sid had been keeping *cave* for Wilberforce in case any of the morning's hunters should return. Now the rats were crouched in the scuppers, their backbones sharply etched, with every hair on end, like a fine-toothed comb, and the noise – kitch-er, kitch-er, kitch! – spat between bared teeth. Immediately, Bowler and Brolly arched their backs and spat their challenge in return – ps-ss-ss! Two pairs of fiery red eyes blazed down at two pairs of angry emerald slits.

Wilberforce looked from the lighter to the jetty and back again. Of course, he realised that cats and rats aren't always the best of friends, but this instant hostility disappointed him.

'Now, Sid, my cheery old China!' he began.

'Kitch-er, kitch-er, kitch!'

'Oh, come along . . .! Flo, then. . .?'

'Kitcher-er, kitch!'

'Oh dear . . .! Well, Mr Brolly, can I appeal to you . . .?'

'Mer-ra-ow!'

'Mr Bowler?'

'Mer-ra-ow!'

'But you mustn't be like this . . .! You can't . . .! Look!'

Then, with a flash of inspiration, Wilberforce started to rumble:

> 'We're all pals together,
>   Comrades and friends are we,
> The more we stick together,
>   The merrier we shall be,'

and the whale was so disarming that, by the end of the chorus, backbones and tempers had quite begun to subside. 'And just once more, *if* you please . . .

> 'We're all pals together.

All together now . . .

> 'Pom-pom-pom friends are we. . . .'

And much to their own surprise, Flo and Sid found themselves polka-ing round J. F. Hogband's capstan, while Bowler and Brolly threw an arm across each other's shoulders and broke into an elegant soft-shoe shuffle.

In the middle of all this, Hercules woke up with a yawn.

'Haw! What's all this haw-horrid row? Can't a chap have his beauty sleep?'

'Ah!' beamed Wilberforce. 'Allow me to introduce Hercules, my steamy, super-heated, reciprocating old tug-friend with Sid and Flo on board, and my two associates. . . .'

'Ps-ss-ss! They mustn't guess who!'

But solid old Hercules seemed to be the final straw in the balance, and though a certain reserve remained between the two parties – the rats keeping carefully within the safety of J.F.H.'s coamings – Bowler and Brolly allowed themselves to be introduced and even, with a little further persuasion, revealed the dark secret of the threatened theft of the Crown Jewels.

'But no one knows exactly when this 'ere mob's goin' to 'alf-inch the jools,' said Sid, 'the Crown and Sceptre?'

'Nobody except the gang,' said Wilberforce.

'Haw, haw!' laughed Hercules. 'No one knows

when they're going to steal the *sceptre* ex-*sceptre* gang! Haw-haw-haw!'

'Erky-boy likes his jokes simple,' grinned Sid.

'Haw-aw-aw,' sighed Hercules and went back to sleep.

'Well, as I was saying, dear fellow,' Brolly picked up the thread of their discussion, 'as I was saying when our friends, Sidney and Florence, appeared, I think it was the topper. . . .'

'Just a touch too swagger,' explained Bowler.

'So, if you could see your way to. . . .'

'But of course,' Wilberforce agreed. 'It's as easy as swallowing cuttlefish. All I have to do to make it go is just to wish,' and – pop! – the top hat and monocle simply disappeared.

'Splendid!' beamed Brolly, 'but the trouble is, that, since half London has been out hunting you, you're rather well known.'

'Which means,' added Bowler, 'that from now on you'll have to go about in disguise.'

'Disguise! Oo-ooh!' said Wilberforce, thrilled.

'An impenetrable disguise, dear fellah,' said Brolly, 'for which, by good fortune, I have brought the necessary *impedimenta*.' And with a theatrical gesture he swept off his bowler hat and produced from inside it a black-japanned tin box and a lot of what looked like tousled hair.

'Me make-up, laddie,' Brolly purred. 'You can trust me for the make-up! Seven seasons in the lead with Dick Whittington,' he went on, and his voice seemed to have acquired a new, plummy richness.

Wilberforce caught a glance between Flo and Sid. It was a questioning look. Some private thought had passed between them, but he couldn't fathom what it was.

'Yes, laddie – the Cat's Whiskah of Radio, Stage and Screen,' Brolly went on. '"Star" on me dressing-room door! Me public queuing for me autograph! Such was *fame*, dear fellah!'

'On with the motley, my friend!' exclaimed Bowler, striking an attitude.

'The paint and the powder!' added Brolly.

And before he realised what was happening, Wilberforce found the two cats pattering about on his head and setting to work at his disguise. Soft paws smoothed sticks of coloured greasepaint over his face while the cats intoned a sort of ritual chorus.

'Foundation cream!' called Brolly.

'Foundation cream!' replied Bowler, handing a tin of white grease, which they spread over his face.

'Five, nine and powder!'

'Five, nine and powder!'

It was mumbo-jumbo and high cock-a-lorum to Wilberforce, but the two theatrical cats seemed to know what they were talking about and daubed his face all over with coloured grease.

'Spirit gum!'

'Spirit gum!'

There was a moist dab on Wilberforce's upper lip, which stung a little.

'Moustache!'

'Moustache!'

Something tickly was pressed above his mouth.

'Beard!'

'Beard!'

There was pressure on his chin, and an elastic snapped on the top of his head.

At this point Wilberforce again caught a glimpse of Flo and Sid, and again the questioning glance passed between them.

'Wig!' called Brolly.

'Wig!' replied Bowler. Then, 'How's that for a quick change, laddie?'

'His own mother wouldn't know him,' added Brolly, producing a travelling mirror, which he held so that Wilberforce could see what he looked like.

Wilberforce stared at the mirror. There was a long silence.

'Does it come off?' he asked.

'A touch of removal cream, and it's gone!'
'Oh!'

And then the whale began to chuckle – ha ha! – The George Robey eyebrows! Ha-ha-ha! – the curly, blond wig! Ha-ha-ha-ha-ha! – the Charlie Chaplin moustache! Ho-ho-ho-ho! – And the big bushy beard with the complexion of a half-fried Red Indian! – Ha-ha-ha, Ho-ho-ho!

'Oh dear, oh dear!' cried Wilberforce, tears of laughter pouring from his eyes.

Sid and Flo, too, were rolling on their backs on the deck, kicking their legs in the air.

'Oh, please stop it, do! It hurts,' cried Flo holding her sides. 'Oh dear, oh dear!'

And even Bowler and Brolly, who looked a bit put out at first, ended by joining in the laughter.

Then suddenly disaster struck. Panting and laughing, Wilberforce drew in a deep breath. As he did so, the bushy beard curled upwards towards his mouth and disappeared – ff-ff-flup! The whale gave a cough. The terrific intake of air had sucked the beard down his throat just like a hoover, and there it was, stuck fast.

Wilberforce coughed, gasped, wheezed and coughed again. Even under his Red Indian make-up you could see his face growing redder and redder. He couldn't get a proper breath.

''Ere,' cried Sid starting to look worried, 'it's the Barnet Fair!'

'It's the hair,' gasped Wilberforce.

'Didn't I say Barnet Fair?'

'It's stuck in 'is billy,' said Flo.

'My throat,' came a worried wheeze.

'Your billy goat, that's it,' said Sid.

'Don't stand there talking,' said Flo. 'We must *do* something.'

'Try and push it right down with a mop,' suggested Brolly.

'Send for the Fire Brigade,' said Bowler.

Meanwhile, heaving and gasping for breath, Wilberforce was growing redder and redder and redder. Then. . . .'

''Old it. Wilby-boy! 'Old it!' cried Sid. 'Open your mouth as wide as you can and 'old it!'

Wilberforce did his best to obey. Then, with heroic courage, the brave rat sprang from the taffrail into the vast cavern and disappeared – whee-ee-ee-ee!

'Cor! It ain't 'alf dark in 'ere!' his voice echoed.

'A-ha!' coughed Wilberforce.

'Eh! Not so much of the corf! You blown me 'alf-way back to start. Nar then, I can just feel a corner. . . .'

'A-ha!' Wilberforce coughed again.

'Nah, Wilby-boy, 'old on!'

'But you're tickling worse and worse,' wheezed the whale.

'I don't care. You *must* 'old on. Now, 'ere it is, I think. . . . Yes, that's it. . . . Nar, a good strong pull and. . . .'

'A-ha, ha-ha a-a-a-ah!' – Wilberforce's control gave out with one huge cough, and with that cough, like a human cannon-ball in a circus, Sid shot right out into the river – whee-ee-ee-ee! – triumphantly brandishing in his forepaws . . . the beard.

'Oh, thank goodness! And thank you, Sid,' cried Wilberforce, taking in a grateful breath of air. And then he went on, 'I don't think I really *want* to be disguised, if you please.'

'But your secret instructions are on the way,' objected Bowler.

'Tomorrow,' hissed Brolly.

'Well, I'll hide till then,' said Wilberforce, and – blabble - ebble - ibble - obble - ubble! – he submerged under the broad keel of J.F.H.

6

Secret Instructions

In the end, Wilberforce didn't have to stay hidden under J.F.H. very long, because early next morning Hercules steamed off and fetched Buttercup, another of Bella's sisters, and when he got back he moored her with Bella and Primrose to make a square on the side of the jetty like a private swimming pool, where the whale could float on the surface and chat with his friends without being seen.

Wilberforce was very grateful. Being in hiding wasn't much fun. Well, you know what it's like in hide-and-seek when you get a place that's a bit *too* good, and people don't find you; it gets jolly dull. Well, that's how Wilberforce felt. So as soon as he heard Sid's cheery voice calling:

'All clear, Wilby-boy! Up you come!' he surfaced right away – blubble-ibble-abble-swoosh!

'Oh, that's much better, thanks,' he grinned.

'Flo's just bringing up the elevenses,' Sid went on. 'Thought you'd like a nice cuppa!'

'There's some like their tea in a saucer,' rumbled Wilberforce, taking in a deep breath of fresh air,

> 'And some like a can for their tea,
> But what I like hot,
> In a steaming pot. . . .'

'Is a nice cup of Rosy Lea,' put in Sid, laughing.

Well, just after Flo had filled the big mugs with 'the best Sergeant Major's, wot you could stand your spoon up in,' Wilberforce noticed an odd thing.

When he had first surfaced there had been one of those red and white striped tent shelters right at the far end of the jetty – the sort the electricity men put over manholes when they're mending the wires under the pavement. Well, *now* the shelter was almost half-way down the jetty, and as he watched Wilberforce felt sure. . . . Yes, there was no doubt about it! . . . the shelter was moving, one might almost say tiptoeing, towards them.

'Look!' said Wilberforce.

'Wot a strerorinary thing,' said Sid.

'I never seen the like,' said Flo.

With growing curiosity the three of them watched, as every so often the red and white shelter moved itself forward a few paces and then stopped, as if it were pretending it was an ordinary shelter standing over an ordinary manhole. Then, rather stealthily, it would ease itself forward again until, in a final conspiratorial slither, it came to rest level with Bella's bow. Then, as the three friends watched fascinated, the crook of an umbrella appeared through the opening at the front and pulled the canvas sharply to one side.

'Mr Bowler!' exclaimed Wilberforce.

'Ps-ss-ss! We aren't here!' whispered Bowler looking out cautiously.

'You haven't seen us!' added Brolly, appearing over his shoulder.

The two cats looked swiftly up and down the jetty and, seeing no one about, stalked stealthily out.

'We bring you,' whispered Brolly, 'your secret instructions.'

'Ooh-ooh!' said Wilberforce excitedly.

'At some time after dark tomorrow . . .' Bowler took up the tale.

'Probably about midnight . . .' Brolly chipped in.

'The thieves will leave the Tower with their booty.'

'The thieves ... er, yes,' said Wilberforce. 'What will they be like? I mean, will they be very fierce...? Er ... I mean, how many...?'

'Ps-ss-ss! Nobody knows,' chorused the two cats.

'They will leave,' Brolly lowered his voice even further and looked furtively over his shoulder, 'they will leave by ... Traitors' Gate!'

'Er Traitors' Gate ... naturally!' Wilberforce nodded.

'A path leads from this gate to the river. ...'

'Where a boat will be waiting for them.'

'You will take up a suitable concealed position for observing the whole scene. ...'

'And arrest them as they emerge.'

'But if I don't know who they are,' put in Wilberforce, 'how shall I know whom to arrest?'

'Ps-ss-ss! We leave the details to you,' hissed Brolly, slithering back into the canvas tent.

'This shelter,' added Bowler following him, 'will self-destruct in fifteen seconds,' and he flipped the entrance to with the crook of his umbrella. Then the red and white striped shelter picked itself up, as it were, and slithered rapidly to the landward end of the jetty, where it set itself down again.

Immediately, the two cats slipped out under the canvas and disappeared round one of the warehouses. The next instant the shelter burst into flames. As it burnt rapidly down, a puff of wind blew it over the side of the jetty. There was a hiss as it touched the water, and then it sank, leaving nothing to show that it had ever existed except a small cloud of smoke, and a minute later even that had faded away.

'Coo-er!' said Wilberforce, his eyes fairly popping out of his head. 'That was the real thing!'

Then he started swimming excitedly backwards and forwards in his pool between the barges.

'Planning!' he muttered, 'We must prepare plans at once. This means careful thought.'

'Usin' the loaf, eh?' said Sid.

'Loaf?' queried the whale.

'Loaf of bread,' Flo prompted.

'Oh – head! Yes, we must certainly use our loaf.' Wilberforce frowned in deep concentration. 'Now let me see. . . . First, as to equipment . . . er supplies, er paraphernalia . . .' and now he was almost marching up and down his pool. Indeed, if he could only have put his fins behind his back, you could have mistaken him for Napoleon. '. . . Yes, equipment . . . a torch, of course, compass, tape measure, handcuffs, finger-print outfit

... and all that sort of thing. Perhaps Flo can go down to the supermarket and do some shopping for us. ... Then, as to communications – do you understand semaphore, Sid, my cipher-solving little signaller? Or perhaps we could use morse code with the torch. ...'

Sid looked a bit nonplussed.

'First we must scout out the site – forward planning, you see. ... But that raises the main difficulty, the heart of the matter, the – er – nub, as you might say. It all depends on my – er not being recognised, preferably not even seen. ... I mean, yesterday's attempts at disguise were not very. ...'

'Not at *all*,' Flo put in, and all three of them smiled for a moment at the thought of Wilberforce's extraordinary appearance.

'Wilby-boy,' said Sid thoughtfully, 'them two, Bowler and Brolly, 'ave you ever met 'em before? I mean, do you know anything about 'em?'

'Well, they come from the – er "Sh-sh-sh, you mustn't say who!" – you know, the Secret Service.'

'You're sure?'

'They told me so themselves,' Wilberforce replied stoutly. 'Now, let's get on with the master plan, the – er key. ...'

'If you say so, Wilby-boy!'

'Now the whole point is that I mustn't be spotted.'

'Haw-aw!' said Hercules quietly. 'If you don't want to be spotted, see you don't catch measles! Haw-haw-haw!' he guffawed.

'Oh Hercules!' everyone groaned, and then, 'Stop hooting!'

And Sid had to cut off his steam in case his laughter should be mistaken for distress signals and lead other ships to discover where Wilberforce was hiding.

'Thank you, Sid,' the whale resumed. 'But although theatrical disguise won't do, I think one of my Aunty Barnacle's runes might help.'

And before anyone could say a word – blabble-ibble-ubble! – he had dived under Bella, where he could be heard muttering intently. Then there came the usual 'ching,' and – blubble-ibble-abble! – he came up wearing a felt hat with the brim snapped low over his eyebrows and a silk scarf across the lower half of his face.

'You don't know who I am now, do you?' he asked Flo.

'You're Wilberforce, dearie,' she replied.

'Oh!' said Wilberforce crestfallen, and – pop! – the hat and scarf were wished away.

'Make-up no good! Disguise no good! And I'm too big, er . . . too far round the gas works to hide!' sighed the whale. 'So what do we do?'

'If you was only a chameleon, you could change colour,' said Flo.

'But that's it! Of course, that's it! Camouflage!' cried Wilberforce enthusiastically. 'Camouflage me as something large and moist like a . . . like a. . . .'

'A mud flat,' suggested Sid.

'The very thing! You cover me all over with mud. . . . Of course, it'll take a bit of time.'

'No it won't,' cried Sid excitedly. "Alf a jiff!'

And he skipped off down the jetty as fast as he could. At the shore end he put a paw to his mouth and gave a piercing whistle. Almost immediately, four or five other rats came running out of the nearby warehouses, and Wilberforce could see Sid talking earnestly to them.

"E's calling out the Reserves! . . . Emergency!' explained Flo.

And so it was that five minutes later, three or four hundred rats, no less, were scuttering down the jetty – big rats, little rats, brown, grey and piebald, young and fat, lean and skinny, and even one very old fellow with a wooden leg and a crutch.

'Percy Pegg,' Flo pointed out the old veteran

with admiration, 'served forty years in the Volunteers and never missed a call or a reunion supper in all them days!'

Sid stood up on J. F. Hogband's counter issuing orders, and in no time at all several rat-chains were passing mud from paw to paw along the jetty to the basin, where dozens of other rats were spreading it over Wilberforce's ample back.

'I'm having a mud-pack,' grinned the whale. 'So good for the complexion!'

Very soon he was almost completely covered, and he really did look very like a mudbank as the tide goes out, except that two intelligent eyes twinkled through the holes that had been left for them. Just the last square yard in the middle of his back awaited completion while, rather heavily, and a bit soggily, Wilberforce floated there.

Only one rat remained aboard to deal with this final space. A load of mud was passed down, and the whale's body sank a tiny inch lower in the water; another load, and another tiny inch down ... another ... and then ... there was a noise like a bath emptying – sker-er-ertch! – the single rat still aboard gave a terrified squeak, scurried to the jetty, scrabbled at the wood with his paws, and only just managed to scramble ashore to safety with the help of two friends, as

Wilberforce – sker-er-ertch! – sank slowly and gently – sker-er-ertch! – like a submarine – blobble-obble-obble! – and disappeared out of sight.

The load of mud had been too heavy for him!

7

Traitors' Gate

And so Wilberforce sank under the weight of the mud. Of course, it didn't worry him in the least. In fact he only stayed down for half a minute, but when he re-surfaced, four hundred rat faces fell as one. The whale's back which had just been so carefully disguised as a mudbank was now as clean as a whistle. The water had washed all the mud away, and with it a whole afternoon's work. Wilberforce looked over his shoulder.

'Oh dear!' he murmured. 'Oh dear, I *am* sorry, chaps!'

'Nah! Nah!' put in Sid good-humouredly. 'Not to bovver! Look at it this way, Wilby-boy. 'Ow many is there goin' to be in this 'ere gang of villains tomorrow night?'

'That's what's so worrying,' replied Wilberforce. 'I don't know.'

'Well, suppose there's two of them . . . suppose there's six of them . . . suppose there's an organised gang – and the whole plot's that desperate – and suppose they're all armed to the teeth, wouldn't you be glad to 'ave three or four 'undred Volunteer Rat Reserves be'ind you?'

'By jove yes!' said Wilberforce. 'They'd make all the difference.'

'Then, all you Reserve boys,' called Sid, turning to the crowd on the jetty, 'all you Reservists take them crestfallen looks off your hugly mugs, and stand by for some *real* action after dark tomorrow evening.'

The whole band cheered and turned about and, with Percy Pegg stomping his wooden leg at their head, they jostled good-humourcdly down the jetty towards the warehouses from which they had come.

'What a splendid idea of yours, Sid!' said Wilberforce appreciatively, 'Most heartening, er . . . reassuring, to feel your Special Reserves are standing by in case of any difficulty! Not, of course, that they will be needed, but just in case of the eventuality, er . . . contingency, er . . . any little thing going wrong. . .!'

'Delighted to be of 'elp,' said Sid.

'Now, about this Recce, this scouting the

terrain,' Wilberforce went on, 'I really *must* find some way to make myself invisible.'

'Haw-aw! Try vanishing cream!' hooted Hercules, 'Haw-haw-haw!'

'Oh, Hercules!' everybody groaned, and Sid went on,

'Now, 'Erky-boy, what 'ave you started talking for? You know you're not let, except in fog.'

'Haw-haw! You've been so busy talking and planning yourselves, you haven't noticed the splendid haw-haze haw-hanging about.'

And it was true. A light haze was hovering in wispy clouds above the river, thickening as the sun dipped towards the city roofs and the evening chill set in.

'So I can talk as much as I like,' said Hercules smugly, 'and if I can't find anything else to say, I shall recite my multiplication tables from two-times right through to twelve . . . so!'

'You wouldn't know 'ow, 'Erky-boy,' laughed Sid. 'Wot's two elevens?'

'Twenty-three,' replied Hercules promptly.

'Twenty-two, 'Erky-boy,' Sid corrected.

'That's that *you* think. *My* eleven always travels with a reserve. Haw-haw-haw-haw-haw!'

''Erky-boy, you get worse and worse,' they all laughed.

'Haw-aw! Who's the clever one here, then? Who wastes time talking about disguises? If the villains are going to do the crime after dark, nobody can be seen, so who *needs* a disguise? And the same goes for your-haw Recce – no one will see you in this mist.'

'But *that*, my perceptive, my perspicacious tug friend,' said Wilberforce admiringly, 'is *brains*!'

And Sid added: "Erky-boy, I'll never say you're slow again.'

'Well then,' said Wilberforce, 'what are we waiting for?' and he did a neat duck dive under Primrose, out into the main stream.

The mist was ideal and gave a visibility of only twenty or thirty yards. So if Wilberforce kept low in the water, he was unlikely to be seen by anyone unless they were very close, when of course he could just do a shallow dive and disappear.

In no time at all Hercules had thrown off his lines, and they were all chugging upstream towards the red lights which marked the level of the roadway across the bridge. Hercules was stubby enough to get underneath without asking for the bascules to be raised, but he pulled his smoke stack down just for safety and let it spring upright again as soon as they were through. Wilberforce followed a few yards astern, and immediately on

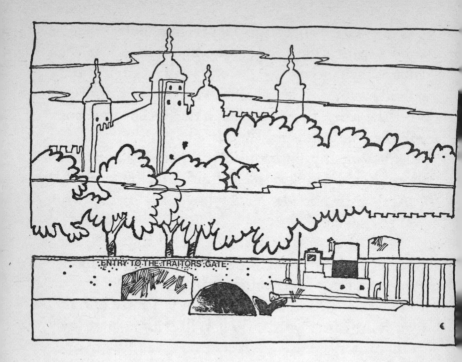

ENTRY TO THE TRAITORS GATE

entering the next reach they turned to starboard and the Tower, heading for a gateway in the middle of its curtain wall.

The massive arch had a forbidding air and seemed doubly mysterious viewed through the wispy fog. The ponderous wooden beams of the main gate, and the sharp spikes sticking downwards from the portcullis, stood back in shadow.

'That's it, mate,' said Sid in a half whisper, 'that's Traitors' Gate. The jools is kept in a underground room near the barracks. Goodness knows 'ow the villains is goin' to get them out!'

'And there's the Bloody Tower just be'ind it, where all them kings and queens was put,' added Flo, and she, too, spoke in a whisper.

It was not just that they didn't want to draw attention to themselves, but the mist hanging below this frowning fortress awed them into lowered voices.

Briefly they glimpsed a yeoman warder pass behind the grille, but instead of the scarlet Beefeater's rig of State occasions he was in his 'blues', and his drabness accentuated the ominous threat contained in those two terrible words, 'Traitors' Gate'. Wilberforce shivered, and a momentary silence fell over them.

'What about the plan, Wilby-boy?' Sid murmured.

'Well, it looks straightforward enough,' replied Wilberforce in a business-like voice. 'You tow Bella and Marigold down by that raft of barges opposite. Then I'll submerge between them, just keeping my eyes level with the water, and you can stand by with Hercules. He'll have to dowse his riding lights of course.'

At this point they were interrupted by a single hoarse 'kark!' Within the dark cavern of the gate's mouth appeared the tattered black figure of a large raven, hopping slowly forward and flapping ungainly wings to keep his balance.

'Kark!' repeated the bird, cocking a beady eye in their direction. Huddled amongst those rusty, ruffled feathers he looked like an old-fashioned schoolmaster wrapped in his gown.

'That's one of the ravens what they keeps in the Tower,' explained Sid in a whisper. 'It's like a 'istorical memento. They clips their wings so they can't escape. I think this one is the one they calls Edward. 'E's the oldest of the lot, and they do say as 'e's got second sight.'

Edward hopped a little towards them and flapped his stubby wings again.

'Kark!' he cried a third time.

'If 'e's got second sight, why not ask 'im if he can help us wiv this 'ere lark about the Crown Jools?' suggested Flo.

'And for why not?' said Sid and turned towards the raven.

'Mornin', Edward,' he began. The old bird cocked an eye at him severely. 'I mean, good morning, *Mister* Edward,' Sid corrected himself. 'We was wondering like, sir . . . I mean, seeing as 'ow you 'as the gift of second sight, we was thinkin', sir . . .'

  ' "Kark-kark! Unto
    My answer hark," rasped the raven.
  "The villains on their crime embark
  'Neath fitful moon when all is dark.
    Who then shall know
    Which is friend and which is foe?
  Kark-kark! Do you
  This warning mark!" '

and the old bird flapped off, rustling his feathers drily.

The advice seemed so useless that Hercules let out a great, 'Haw-haw!'

At once the raven wheeled round and fixed him with an unwinking stare. He stood there for some seconds. Then, in silence, he turned and flapped away.

'I 'ope you didn't offend the old bird,' said Flo. 'Looks like 'e was trying to put "the eye" on you, 'Erky-boy.'

'Haw-aw!' said Hercules. 'I don't reckon much to his advice.'

'Nor me,' said Sid. 'He looks at you with them two beady mince pies like he wanted to see right through you and then 'e comes out with all this Betty Martin about not recognising people in the dark. Well, I mean to say ...! Still, I hope he didn't cast no spell, 'Erky-boy. You never know what these queer old birds can do!'

'Oh, come on!' said Wilberforce. 'Let's get back to the jetty.'

So Hercules put his engines into reverse – ying-ying-ying! – but nothing happened. So he speeded up a bit – ying-ing-ing-ing-ing! – and then he went full astern – ying-ng-ng-ng-ng! – and *still* nothing happened.

'Haw-aw! I can't move,' he groaned heaving with all his power. 'I'm stuck. Edward has put a spell on me!'

'Your propeller's stirring up a lot of mud,' said Wilberforce. 'You're stranded.'

And it was true. The tide had fallen, and poor Hercules had his bows firmly stuck in the mud.

'Haw-aw! Edward did it for revenge,' moaned the tug, pulling with all his engines. 'Oh, the disgrace! Haw-aw! Haw-aw! A London tug stranded in his own water, haw-aw! I shall be laughed out of the docks, haw-aw! Oh dear, haw-haw-haw!' And he cut his engine and lay there, disconsolate. Poor tubby Hercules was too dispirited and ashamed to say another word.

Then Wilberforce had an idea.

'Lower my under-water motor bike please, Sid,' he said.

'I don't think you'll tow 'im off wiv that,' said

the rat. 'I mean to say, it ain't that powerful.'

'Just you wait and see, my rueful little rodent,' grinned the whale.

So Sid and Flo lowered the bike, and Wilberforce took the handlebars in his mouth and, with the engine turned to half, set off upstream, disappearing very quickly in the mist.

'What's he up to?' asked Flo.

But before Sid could reply, they began to get an answer to their question. Down towards them came the noise of Wilberforce's bike running at full power on the surface. A moment later he came into view adding the thrust of his great fluke tail – per-rump-ah! – to that of the double-throttle red button. As he came downstream, they could see a mighty bow wave building up under his nose.

'I got it!' cried Sid. "E's going to wash us off!'

And then Wilberforce's wave hit them, and the water flooded in, lifting them quite clear of the mud. The boat rocked, righted itself and, with Hercules's engines full astern, pulled safely into mid-stream.

'Haw-ray!' cried Hercules. Indeed they all cheered.

Wilberforce turned the red button off and slowed down.

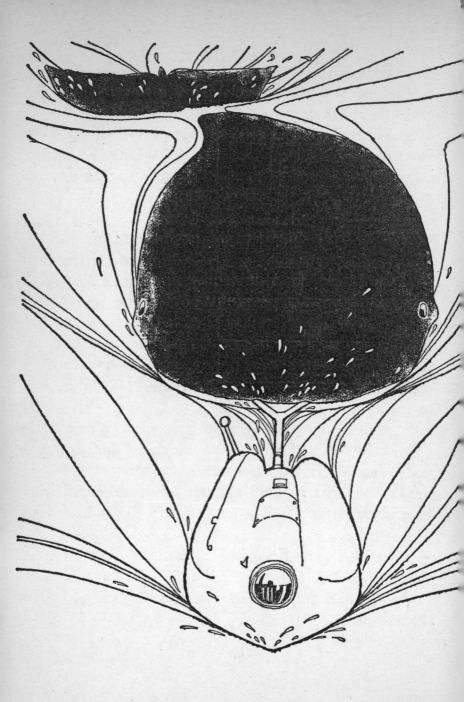

'Follow me home,' he called.

And with a 'Haw-aw! Well done, Wilberforce, and thank you,' from Hercules, tug and whale set off through the mist back to the jetty.

8

The Villains Foiled

A sickle moon hung above the White Tower, throwing deep shadows along the wharf and among the raft of barges where Wilberforce was already in position between Bella and Primrose. From time to time, passing clouds blotted out its pale rays, leaving only a dim owl-light. But even in the darkness, the whale could sense a patch of deeper black that marked the cavernous arch of infamy, Traitor's Gate.

It had been a long and impatient day of waiting, but now they were ready, and with beating heart Wilberforce lay poised to put his detective master plan into action. Like all brilliant military manœuvres, it was essentially simple. As soon as the thieves tried to make their get-away, Hercules would cut them off astern while Wilberforce threw himself across their bows and made the arrest.

'You O.K., Wilby-boy?' Sid whispered, making one of his periodic visits on tiptoe across the barges' decks.

'O.K.!' Wilberforce whispered back. 'Anything to report?'

'Nuffink so far,' said Sid and, with an encouraging thumbs up sign, slipped silently back to his post.

A City church chimed the quarter. Wilberforce lay motionless, watching . . . and thinking. He was puzzled.

All that long day of waiting he had expected a visit from Bowler and Brolly. Flo had served innumberable cups of Rosie Lea from the large metal teapot, and the brews had grown blacker and blacker as time wore on. But it was not until supper that anything happened. J.F.H. had just returned from a visit to the warehouse, and as a result Flo had been able to knock up a particularly delicious supper of banana and coconut, when Wilberforce noticed a street-cleaner at work at the far end of the jetty. He was pushing a pair of dustbins on wheels, and, as Wilberforce watched, the lid of the nearer bin eased upwards, and he was sure he could see a black, bowler-hatted head peering towards him. Then the other bin-lid opened, and this time there was no doubt at all –

the top was being propped up by an umbrella. Wilberforce had spouted a friendly jet of recognition through his blow-hole, and immediately both lids had been slammed shut. It was as if the cats were watching him and didn't want to be seen.

Then there was Edward's warning: 'Which is friend and which is foe?' ... What did it all mean?

The church clock chimed again, this time the full hour, and immediately after, from within the Tower itself, came the well-known challenge:

'Halt! Who comes there?'

'The keys!'

'Whose keys?'

'The Queen's keys!'

The Tower was being locked up for the night.

Time hung and hung. And then the church clock spoke again. Twelve notes rang out across the still river towards a Tower Bridge now deserted of traffic. Midnight! And as the last bell tolled, almost as if it had been stage-managed, a large cloud swept across the moon, plunging the scene into total blackness.

Wilberforce peered into the dark. Were there figures moving on the wharf below the Byward Tower? And in that direction, towards the Lanthorn Tower, were those shadowy shapes real? Wilberforce tensed himself. Then the cloud drifted on, the moon's rays started to filter back, and the whale saw for the first time what he was up against!

On the whaft to one side was ranged a platoon of the Guards, to the other a posse of Beefeaters. But they were not armed, as you would have expected, with truncheons and handcuffs; instead they carried nets and harpoons! The whale gulped in horror. They were not looking for the thieves, they were looking for *him*, Wilberforce! And at the same instant the sound of powerful engines – br-rr-rm, br-rr-rm – moving fast upstream revealed six river-police launches in formation, spearheading the hunt. And then, as the full moon returned, the whole infamous plot became clear to him.

'Wilby-boy!' Sid's instant whisper sounded beside him, 'it's a double-cross!'

'I know,' said Wilberforce, 'but there's something else as well. Listen!' and he started whispering urgently in Sid's ear.

'But o' course! Fancy us not seein' that!' replied Sid. 'Now, if Flo and I . . .' and his voice sank to an even more hushed whisper as he started to outline plans.

'Agreed!' nodded Wilberforce. 'My job's clear, of course, but as for Hercules. . . .'

'Oh, 'Erky-boy's on for certain. You can count on that,' said Sid and vanished like a ghost.

The next instant, a searchlight mounted on one of the turrets flashed down among the barges quartering the river in a threatening probe. Wilberforce crash-dived – perra-blompf!

Safely under water, the whale heard Hercules start his engines and move off upstream. His riding lights, Wilberforce knew, were dowsed, and this suspicious movement immediately caught the attention of the river-police who set off in instant pursuit with sirens blaring – hoo-erp, hoo-erp, hoo-erp! Looking up to the surface above his nose, Wilberforce saw four little legs kicking vigorously through the water. It was Sid on his way to land. . . . Would he be in time?

The searchlight's finger wavered across the river. Twice its circle of light hesitated on the surface above Wilberforce's head. Then it thrust far upstream and finally went out altogether.

Cautiously, Wilberforce put one eye at water level. In the distance the police boats' sirens pursued Hercules beyond London Bridge, and half-way up the Pool several boats loaded with

Guardsmen and Beefeaters were rowing after them as hard as they could.

Suddenly, there was a noise to make your blood run cold – mer-aow-er-aow-er-aow! – and on to the battlements sprang two black figures silhouetted against the moon. One wore a bowler hat, and the other carried an umbrella, and both were unmistakably cats. Swiftly along the walls they fled, and then pell-mell behind them poured rats and rats and rats – the Reserves were out in force! In the lead was a figure which he was sure was Sid's, and next, brandishing his crutch, was Percy Pegg running as fast on his three good legs as anyone else could on four.

The caterwauling was indescribable, as the four hundred rats chased Bowler and Brolly round and round the walls. At length the cats sprang down to ground level and disappeared from view, but Wilberforce could hear the pursuit moving east. A moment later the hue and cry reappeared at Tower Bridge. Here the Reserves drew to a halt, whilst the two cats slunk forward, and for a moment Wilberforce was afraid they were going to be allowed to escape. Then Percy Pegg whirled his crutch three times round his head and let go. Whiz-z-z-z-z! – it sailed through the air, and – boink! – hit Bowler behind the ear. As he stumbled,

Brolly tripped over him. At the same instant, a small but widening gap appeared half-way along the Bridge. Sid was opening it!

The cats gathered themselves together and started to scramble up the ever-increasing slope; but by the time they reached the top there was quite a big gap between the two halves. Brolly leapt and, clutching his bowler hat, just landed, teetering, on the far edge, but Bowler, a second behind, saw that for him the leap had become too great. The bascules continued winding upwards, and there were the two cats treed, one on each half of the bridge, unable to go any higher and too terrified to come down.

Meanwhile, in the river below, Wilberforce had eased out to midstream, where the re-approaching sound of sirens told him that brave old Hercules had doubled about and was leading the police back. Aloft, Bowler and Brolly wobbled, petrified at the height. Suddenly, Brolly, who was waving his hat to keep balance, gave a lurch, and out of the famous bowler, where it had been hidden, fell a large jewelled circlet that glistened in the moonlight. At the same time, a long, straight object slipped gleaming from its hiding place in Bowler's brolly. It was the Crown and Sceptre!

Slowly it seemed, at first, the Crown Jewels hovered, then, gathering speed, they plunged into the water just as the first police launch drew level. With a 'splash' the priceless regalia vanished below the surface. Like lightning Wilberforce crash-dived – perra-blompf! So brightly did the jewels glitter that he quickly gathered them in his mouth and re-surfaced – blubble-ibble-abble-swoosh! – just next to a police launch, where an inspector leaned over the side and gathered them safely in his hands. Then, in the moonlight, he held the gleaming objects aloft, and at the sight

Beefeaters, Guardsmen and Rat Reserves raised a mighty cheer. Then the inspector took from his pocket a big medal on a chain inscribed, *For Work with Intelligence*, and this he hung round Wilberforce's neck, patting him as he did so by way of congratulation because, of course, being a human, he couldn't talk properly.

'That, my furry little fellow detectives,' laughed Wilberforce later, when they had returned to the jetty, 'that was a chase to end all chases.'

'But wot a rotten trick of them two cats,' put in Flo, 'to tell the p'lice as *you* was goin' to carry off the jools by Traitors' Gate, while all the time they was crawlin' down the ventilation shaft to pinch 'em theirselves!'

'All's well that ends well,' grinned Wilberforce. 'But there's one thing that worries me still.'

'Wot's that?' asked Sid.

'This medal,' Wilberforce replied. 'I think *you* ought to have it, Sid. You led the Reserves.'

'But you was the leader of the whole thing,' said Sid magnanimously.

Wilberforce looked round at Flo, 'Flo,' he said, 'who do *you* think ought to have it?'

'Well,' replied the motherly little body, 'seein' as 'ow you asks me, I think you ought to give it to the one we all really wants to give it to.'

'Which is?'

"Erky-boy!'

'Of course!' laughed Sid and Wilberforce to-gether.

So Wilberforce slipped the chain off, and Sid hung it over Hercules's bows, and if Hercules could have blushed with pride, he certainly would have done so. But as it was, he simply said 'Haw-aw, haw-aw, haw-aw!'

More Beaver Books

We hope you have enjoyed this Beaver Book. Here are some of the other titles:

Wilberforce and the Blue Cave A delightful story for younger readers about Wilberforce the whale and his friends Nelson the crab and Melody the shrimp, who go on holiday to the Mediterranean. By Leslie Coleman, author of *Wilberforce the Whale*, also in Beavers

Read Me Another Story Traditional nursery rhymes and fairy tales mix with new and original material in this delightful collection suitable for the youngest readers or for reading aloud. Selected and edited by Frank Waters

Journey to the Jungle A Beaver original. A hilariously funny collection of stories for the youngest readers concerning the adventures of a bus called Livingstone. Written and illustrated by Donald Bisset, author of *This is Ridiculous*, also in Beavers

Treasure Trove A Beaver original. A collection of stories and poems, games to play and things to make, by Jennifer Curry

Charlie in Trouble Two stories for younger readers by Joy Allen, in which Charlie loses first his new wellington boots and then his front teeth. Illustrated by Caroline Sharpe

Fun to Try A Beaver original. Dozens of problems, puzzles and tricks with words, numbers and pictures for all ages

New Beavers are published every month and if you would like the *Beaver Bulletin* – which gives all the details – please send a large stamped addressed envelope to:

Beaver Bulletin
The Hamlyn Group
Astronaut House
Feltham
Middlesex TW14 9AR

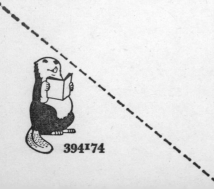

394174